POKÉMON

TEST YOUR SINNOH SMARTS

ULTIMATE QUIZ BOOK

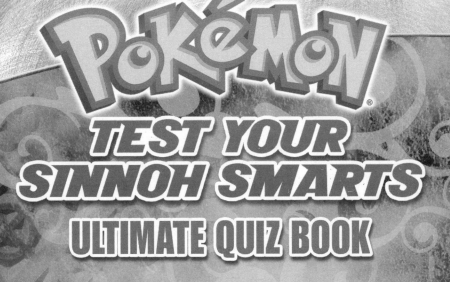

POKÉMON

TEST YOUR SINNOH SMARTS

ULTIMATE QUIZ BOOK

BY CRIS SILVESTRI

SCHOLASTIC INC.

New York   Toronto   London   Auckland   Sydney

Mexico City   New Delhi   Hong Kong   Buenos Aires

No part of this publication may be reproduced, stored in a retrieval system, or transmitted in any form or by any means, electronic, mechanical, photocopying, recording, or otherwise, without written permission of the publisher. For information regarding permission, write to Scholastic Inc., Attention: Permissions Department, 557 Broadway, New York, NY 10012.

ISBN-13: 978-0-545- 09940-0

ISBN-10: 0-545- 09940-4

Published by Scholastic Inc.

12 11 10 9 8 7 6 5 4 3 2 1   9 10 11 12 13 14/0

Cover designed by Henry Ng
Interior designed by Kay Petronio

Printed in the U.S.A.

First printing, February 2009

WELCOME, POKÉMON TRAINERS!

Taking care of Pokémon requires lots of practice, training, and Pokémon-specific knowledge. You'll have to practice and train on your own, but we're here to help with the knowledge.

Contained in these pages are quizzes, puzzles, and trivia based on the *Pokémon: Diamond and Pearl* television show. Some of the questions are definitely for you serious Pokémon viewers — you know, you kids that can't miss an episode, know all the characters, and have seen all the battles.

But there are also lots of activities in here that will test your thinking, just like catching Pokémon in the wild trains your motor skills. Can you spot misspelled Pokémon? How about picking out a Legendary Pokémon from a group of regular Pokémon? How about some Sinnoh Sudoku?

At the end of the book, there's a score chart to see if you truly can move on in your Pokémon training.

Good luck, and remember —

GOTTA CATCH 'EM ALL!

FOLLOWING A MAIDEN'S VOYAGE

PIPLUP

In the Sinnoh Region, Trainers receive their Pokémon from:

- A Professor Oak
- B Professor Pine
- C Professor Rowan

Brrrr! *Piplup can swim in icy northern waters for ten minutes at a time!*

Dawn takes which Pokémon to be her companion?

- A Chimchar
- B Piplup
- C Turtwig

The Professor's lab is in:

- A Lake Verity
- B Jubilife City
- C Sandgem Town

POKÉMON FACT

JAMES
One-third of the notorious Team Rocket, James finds poetry and grace everywhere — until his clumsy bungling of each situation puts his team in peril. He's not very bright, but he is ambitious.

TWO DEGREES OF SEPARATION!

STARLY

Dawn wants to be a great Pokémon Coordinator just like her:

 A   Mom

B   Dad

C   Distant third cousin twice removed

Though small, Starly can flap its wings with great power.

As she trains Piplup, Dawn comes across another Pokémon. That Pokémon is:

A   Starly

B   Pikachu   D   Burmy

C   Buneary   E   All of the above

Where is Team Rocket during all of this? Well, they're . . .

A   Searching for Ash

 B   Relaxing at a vacation house owned by James's family

C   Having Meowth declawed

SINNOH SUDOKU!

HEY, POKÉMON FANS!

Try your hand at the hot puzzle craze called Sudoku — with a Sinnoh twist! Simply look at each 3 x 3 grid and replace every blank with a Pokémon from the list to the right. Remember, no two Pokémon can occupy the same row or column, and they can't be repeated in the same 3 x 3 grid either. Have fun!

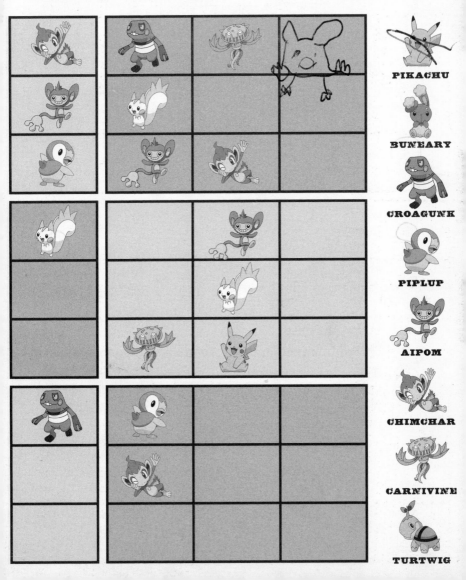

BUDEW

Who is the traveling bard from this episode?

A   William Shakespeare

B   Nando

C   Francis Bacon

The pollen that's released from Budew's bud can cause runny noses and sneezing.

The bard's Pokémon turns out to be:

A   Cherrim

B   Budew

C   Burmy

The first of many exciting Evolutions occurs during this episode. It is:

A   Budew into Roselia

B   Cherubi into Cherrim

C   Burmy into Wormadam

POKÉMON FACT

EVOLUTION
Many Pokémon evolve from one form to another. Some Pokémon have three different stages of Evolution. Typically, the evolved form of a particular Pokémon is more powerful than its earlier form.

GETTIN' TWIGGY WITH IT!

ONIX

Who first makes off with Pikachu in this episode?

- A   Team Rocket
- B   Turtwig
- C   Oddish

Onix can tunnel through the ground at 50 mph.

Who knocks out Ash and Pikachu, and how?

- A   Oddish with Sleep Powder
- B   Professor Plum with the candlestick
- C   Jigglypuff with Sing

Where do our adventurers take a break?

- A   Lake Verity Hot Springs
- B   Sandgem All You Can Eat Buffet
- C   Clara's lakeside home

DIFFERENT STROKES FOR DIFFERENT BLOKES

STANTLER

Ash runs into Paul again, and this time he starts the battle off with:

   A   Pikachu

B   Chimchar

C   Turtwig

It's easy to fall under the spell of Stantler's majestic antlers.

In the forest, Ash comes across a herd of:

   A   Psyduck

B   Fans

C   Stantler

True or False: Ash loses the final battle in this episode.

A   True

   B   False

LIKE IT OR LUP IT!

LUDICOLO

Dawn is desperately training her Piplup for:

A. Attention
B. A Pokémon Contest
C. A Gym Battle

When Ludicolo hears music, its muscles are filled with energy and it has to dance!

Team Rocket initiates a showdown between:

A. Ash and Dawn
B. Dawn and Paul
C. Ludicolo and Golduck

Piplup finally learns a move that will help Dawn in the upcoming contest, and ends up defeating Team Rocket. That move is:

A. BubbleBeam
B. Water Gun
C. Hydro Blast

IT'S A MAP, MAP, MAP WORLD!

If you're serious about becoming a Pokémon Trainer, you have to learn to read a compass. Sinnoh is a large and intimidating place at times, and you could easily get lost. Try your skill reading the directions and see if you can unscramble our message. Remember to follow the steps in order, or you may get confused!

V is South of S and North of E

A is West of S

E is South of A

E is Southeast of S

N is Southwest of A

H is Northwest of R

P is Southeast of R

S is 2 spaces South of H

U is East of S

V is Southwest of V

G is 2 spaces West of V

I is 2 spaces West of E, or Southwest of E

POKÉMON FACT

TRAINER

A human who attempts to capture Pokémon. Children are granted "licenses" to become Pokémon Trainers at the age of ten.

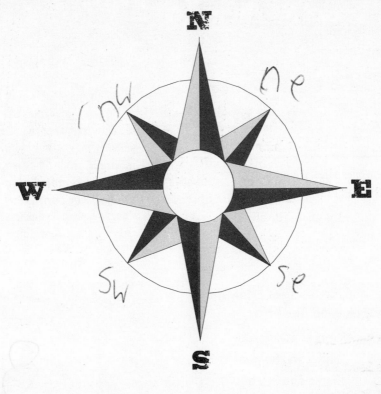

NW NE SW SE

N
E W
S

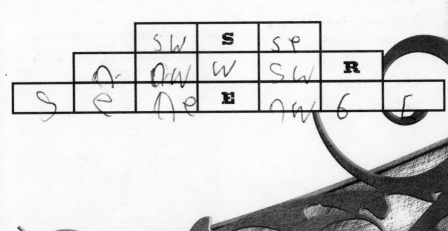

		SW	S	SE		
	A	AW	W	SW	R	
S	e	Ne	E	AW	G	E

GYMBALIAR!

SCIZOR

Scizor uses its huge pincers to intimidate its foes.

Who does Jessie disguise herself as in this episode?

- A   Queen Leafetah
- B   The Jessinator
- C   Princess Powerzone

Ash and friends meet a new Trainer and Pokémon. They are:

- ~~A   Minnie and Mickey~~
- B   Minnie and Scyther
- C   Minnie and Scizor

Brock ends up with a new Pokémon named:

- A   Carnivine
- B   Croagunk
- C   Cranidos

POKÉMON FACT

JESSIE
One-third of the notorious Team Rocket, this sly and sometimes clueless female spy always seems to find the easy way out — which never turns out to be that easy!

SETTING THE WORLD ON ITS BUNEARY!

BUNEARY

In this episode, Dawn uses Piplup's BubbleBeam to fix her:

- A   Car
- B   Hair
- C   Attitude

Buneary unwraps its ears to fight with foes. On chilly nights, it curls up and sleeps with its head buried in its fur.

A Pokémon takes a romantic liking to Pikachu. That Pokémon is:

- A   Pichu
- B   Buneary
- C   Meowth

In a showdown with Dawn, Buneary shows off one of its best moves. That move is:

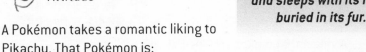

- A   Dizzy Punch
- B   Forest Punch
- C   Fruit Punch

SHINX

A new Pokémon and Trainer appear in this episode. They are:

A) Landis and Shinx
B) Lando and Jynx
C) Misty and Psyduck

When it senses danger, this Pokémon can temporarily blind its foes by creating a dazzling light show with its electrified fur.

The new Trainer's father is:

A) A villain that makes robotic Pokémon
B) The Pokétch Corporation president
C) An evil genius bent on Pokémon domination

Team Rocket have hypnotized the entire Pokémon population of Jubilife City by transmitting:

A) Ralts's psychic energy
B) Jigglypuff's enchanted singing
C) Psyduck's headache-inducing voice

WEAVILE

Weavile uses its super-sharp claws to carve out messages to other Weavile.

Dawn's mother's name is:

 A) Johanna
B Jolene
C Joe Bob Betty Lou

Zoey, one of the Coordinators in the Pokémon Contest, has two Pokémon. They are:

A Skitty and Misdreavus
B Glameow and Misdreavus
 C) Delcatty and Shinx

Jessie assumes yet another wacky identity in this episode. It is:

A Jessaminute
B Shirley U. Jess!
 C) Jessalina

ANAGRAM MADNESS!

Here's a simple one for crafty Trainers! Match the pictures on the right with the anagrams on the left. Some anagrams may actually be more than one word scrambled. Good luck!

ANAGRAM   **SOLUTION**

1. I HACK UP   _blor_ _____

2. ANY RUBE   _____

3. HIS AIR CUP   _____

4. A ROCK GUN   _____

5. TERM TO CAKE   _____

6. CLOUD OIL   _____

7. DIE ELK   _____

8. I A MOP   _____

9. AWARD MOM   _____

10. A VISA RAT   _____

GLAMEOW

Ash is seriously outwitted in the contest with Zoey. Her Glameow wins the creative round after flourishing these two moves:

Glameow may be very fickle, but don't underestimate it. It can put a foe into hypnosis with its stare.

- A   Charm and Captivate
- B   Fake Out and Attract
- **(C)**   Iron Tail and Shadow Claw

The second round of the contest involves:

- A   Dawn and Ash
- **(B)**   Ash and Zoey
- C   Zoey and Dawn

The final round of the contest is between:

- A   Zoey and Jessie
- B   Jessie and Brock
- **(C)**   Ash and Zoey

A STARAVIA IS BORN!

DRAPION

Who monitors the Pokémon that live in the forest near Oreburgh City?

A   Professor Oak
B   Alice
C   Rosebay

Drapion's powerful claws can rip up cars — and they also secrete a powerful poison!

Team Rocket set up a trap to capture flying Pokémon in:

A   Valley Stream
B   Valley Forest
B   Valley Path

Another Evolution occurs during the final fight with Team Rocket. It is:

A   Bonsly into Sudowoodo
B   Hoothoot into Noctowl
C   Starly into Staravia

LEAVE IT TO BROCKO

SUDOWOODO

Ash and friends find Nurse Joy trying to help an injured:

- **A** Shiftry
- **B** Seedot
- **C** Nuzleaf

Despite its wooden appearance, Sudowoodo is more closely related to rocks and stones than trees.

During the breakout from Team Rocket's camp, an Evolution occurs. It is:

- **A** Bonsly into Sudowoodo
- **B** Seedot into Nuzleaf
- **C** Nuzleaf into Shiftry

As Brock coaxes it into a Poké Ball, Sudowoodo has to suddenly fight against its fear of:

- **A** Water
- **B** Fire
- **C** Brock

POKÉMON FACT

NURSE JOY

Nurse Joy is specially trained to treat Pokémon. She works at the Pokémon Center. She is gentle and good-natured, and can treat any Pokémon injury. Like Officer Jenny, she has a number of identical relatives who do the same job as her.

SHAPES OF THINGS TO COME!

BONSLY

Ash is on his way to earn his first Sinnoh Gym Badge in this location:

A   Sandgem Town
B   Oreburgh City
C   Floaroma Town

Bonsly looks like a flower pot with a plant growing out of it, but those green things on top of its head are rocks.

The Gym Leader's name is:

A   Tattoo
B   Herve
C   Roark

The Gym Leader's Pokemon are:

A   Golem, Bastiodon, and Steelix
B   Onix, Marrill, and Elekid
C   Geodude, Onix, and Cranidos

POKÉMON FACT

GYMS
Each town has a Pokémon Gym where potential Trainers ply their craft, learning the ways of the Pokémon before setting out on a journey of discovery.

SINNOH CROSSWORD PUZZLE

Across

1. One of the daughters of the Nurse Joy near Eterna City
3. The Poffin expert of Floaroma Town
6. Brock's new Pokémon
7. Pokémon Hunter J rides this Pokémon
9. Rampardos almost does in Turtwig with this move
10. The new professor in Sinnoh
11. Theresa's aunt
13. This Pokémon has to choose between Dawn and Jessie
14. The final evolved form of Piplup
16. Why Aipom leaves Ash for Team Rocket
19. The Oreburgh City Gym Leader
21. He is a Pokémon bard
22. She monitors Pokémon in the forest near Oreburgh City
23. Another daughter of the Nurse Joy near Eterna City
24. His father is the Pokétch Corporation president

Down

2. The Team Rocket leader
4. Area that Kenny and Dawn are from
5. Piplup learns this move early on
8. Aipom uses this move to send Team Rocket flying
12. The fossils are kept in the Oreburgh _____
15. Dawn's mother
17. *Sinnoh Now!* news team reporter
18. This Pokémon lives near lakes and is made from soil
20. Ash's new rival

A GRUFF ACT TO FOLLOW

CRANIDOS

Cranidos uses its ironclad head to ram into its foes and take them down.

Paul gives away one of his Pokémon for not being tough enough. Which is it?

A   Starly
B   Azumarill
C   Turtwig

Roark's Onix comes into its second battle with Ash and defeats Turtwig:

A   with no remorse
B   with one hit
C   with dignity

Roark looks like he may win again. Which Pokémon does he *not* use?

A   Onix
B   Cranidos
C   Geodude

WILD IN THE STREETS

AERODACTYL

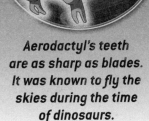

After losing to Roark twice, Ash decides to step up his game, so he trains at the:

- A   Oreburgh Gym
- B   Oreburgh Museum
- **C**   Oreburgh Mines

Aerodactyl's teeth are as sharp as blades. It was known to fly the skies during the time of dinosaurs.

Team Rocket gets a huge surprise when they steal a fossil-restoring machine and ~~_____~~ pops out.

- A   Lileep
- B   Anorith
- **C**   Aerodactyl

We get to witness yet another spectacular Evolution in this episode!

- A   Lileep into Cradily
- **B**   Anorith into Armaldo
- C   Cranidos into Rampardos

RAMPARDOS

Ash decides that the third time's a charm and battles Roark again. In what order does he send his Pokémon to battle?

Rampardos can take down forests with a headbutt that has enough power to knock down even the sturdiest of objects.

  A   Pikachu, Turtwig, Aipom

  B   Turtwig, Aipom, Pikachu

  C   Pikachu, Aipom, Turtwig

Team Rocket try to sneak through the back door of the Oreburgh Gym and steal some Pokémon, only to be thwarted by:

  A   Dawn

  B   Brock

  C   Croagunk

Ash finally takes Roark down and wins his very first badge in Sinnoh: The ⟨Coal⟩ Badge!

  A   Pearl

  B   Diamond

  C   Coal

TWICE SMITTEN, ONCE SHY!

PACHIRISU

At the very beginning of this adventure, Dawn comes across a hyperactive:

A   Staravia

B   Pachirisu

C   Child

Pachirisu lives atop trees and makes electricified fur balls that it hides along with berries it collects.

The newfound Pokémon has to make a choice between:

A   Freedom and captivity

B   Dawn and Jessie

C   Ash and Brock

Team Rocket has a new form of weaponry that it uses to "captivate" Ash and friends. It is:

 A   Stun gun

B   Sticky goo

C   Sleeping charm

EVOLUTION SOLUTION

Put these Pokémon and their evolved forms into the correct order.

1=First Evolution   **2**=Second Evolution   **3**=Third Evolution

For example:

1.

2.

3.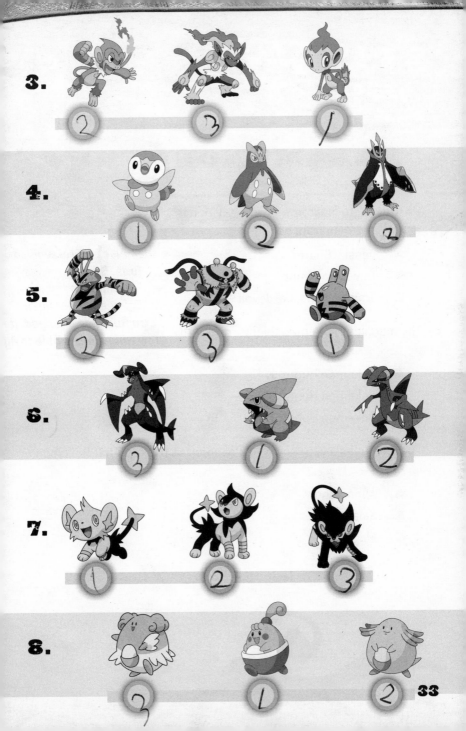

2 3 1

4.

1 2 3

5.

2 3 1

6.

3 1 2

7.

1 2 3

8.

3 1 2

33

MUTINY IN THE BOUNTY!

SALAMENCE

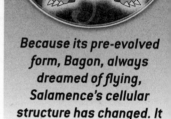

On the way to Floaroma Town, Jessie has a ~~Charm~~ stolen from her.

- (A) Jessie, Charm
- ~~(B)~~ Dawn, Pokémon
- C Trainer Maria, Gardevoir

Because its pre-evolved form, Bagon, always dreamed of flying, Salamence's cellular structure has changed. It grew wings and is able to fly

The merciless Pokémon thief turns out to be:

- A Pokémon Hunter K
- B Pokémon Hunter J
- (C) Pokémon Hunter A

The thief uses a very powerful Pokémon as backup. That Pokémon is:

- A Abomasnow
- (B) Salamence
- C Magikarp

YA SEE WE WANT AN EVOLUTION!

MAGIKARP

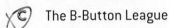

What is the name of the organization that never evolves their Pokémon?

- Ⓐ The Novolvers
- Ⓑ The Floaroma Six
- Ⓒ The B-Button League

Poor Magikarp! It is generally regarded as the weakest Pokémon ever. How it has managed to survive is a mystery.

The leader of this organization is:

- Ⓐ Oralie
- Ⓑ Haley
- Ⓒ Miley

Which two Pokémon from the organization end up defeating Team Rocket?

- Ⓐ Magikarp and Feebas
- Ⓑ Feebas and Pikachu
- Ⓒ Magikarp and Gyarados

BORROWING ON BAD FAITH!

AIPOM

On their way to Floaroma Town, Ash and friends pass a village that's holding an informal Pokémon Contest. What is the prize?

Aipom's tail is more effective than its hands.

- A   A meadow full of flowers
- B   A brand-new Pokémon
- C   A year's supply of fruit

Ash is surprised because one of his Pokémon decides it wants to team up with Team Rocket's Jessie. That Pokémon is:

- A   Pikachu
- B   Turtwig
- C   Aipom

The final round of the contest is a face-off between:

- A   Jessie and Ash
- B   James and Dawn
- C   Dawn and Jessie

BIDOOF

While in the middle of a dig, Team Rocket hits ~~Onix~~ in the ~~tail~~.

- Ⓐ Onix, tail
- Ⓑ Golem, claw
- Ⓒ Steelix, head

Bidoof is more agile than it looks. It will chew on rocks and logs to keep down its sharp teeth.

Ash's group runs from this Pokémon, which has frightened a:

- Ⓐ Gaggle of Girafarig
- Ⓑ Herd of Heracross
- Ⓒ Bunch of Bidoof

The crew must remove something stuck in this Pokémon's head. That item is:

- Ⓐ Ear wax
- Ⓑ Some leftover shovels
- Ⓒ Eye boogers

WORD SEARCH

Can you spot your favorites from Pokémon: Diamond and Pearl in this grid? We know you'll search for them as quickly as if they were in the wild! You can look up, down, forward, backward, and diagonally.

MOTHIM	ABRA	MEOWTH
RHYDON	SHIELDON	SHINX
BEEDRILL	ROSERADE	MISDREAVUS
SANDSHREW	BURMY	GEODUDE
ELECTRIKE	KRICKETUNE	ONIX
MISMAGIUS	PIPLUP	STEELIX
HIPPOPOTAS	ELEKID	SUDOWOODO
SUNFLORA	AIPOM	SHIFTRY
TORTERRA	BUDEW	SEEDOT
BRONZONG	CHERRIM	CRANIDOS
DIALGA	STANTLER	
MURKROW	LUDICOLO	
WEAVILE	SCIZOR	

D	C	I	B	H	B	U	D	E	W	I	G	U	N	N
U	E	R	L	H	N	W	D	T	D	N	O	C	S	U
T	D	Z	H	U	S	U	O	O	O	I	E	P	W	E
U	O	A	X	Y	D	U	D	Z	V	M	A	U	N	W
O	L	D	S	O	D	I	N	A	R	C	O	L	M	E
W	F	E	E	K	K	O	C	F	P	E	H	P	G	E
O	S	G	V	E	R	I	N	O	L	T	P	I	I	A
R	T	I	L	B	S	I	H	E	L	O	A	P	M	A
K	E	E	M	M	A	S	C	I	Z	O	R	G	C	C
R	E	L	T	N	A	T	S	K	D	E	A	A	E	R
U	L	I	L	C	R	N	T	O	E	M	Y	N	I	P
M	I	V	H	I	P	P	O	P	O	T	A	S	C	P
I	X	A	K	A	R	W	R	D	M	M	U	A	C	R
H	E	E	G	C	O	D	T	U	L	V	K	N	U	G
T	P	W	X	D	H	S	E	A	A	E	X	D	E	M
O	G	E	U	M	H	E	R	E	S	A	I	S	W	E
M	Z	S	H	I	F	T	R	Y	B	D	N	H	A	R
E	H	L	N	I	E	D	A	R	E	S	O	R	S	L
A	K	X	M	I	S	M	A	G	I	U	S	E	Y	R
V	A	A	T	I	N	Z	B	U	R	M	Y	W	O	E
D	Y	O	M	E	O	W	T	H	S	R	M	D	C	U

COOKING UP A SWEET STORY

PIKACHU

Who wants to borrow Pikachu for three days?

- (A) Dawn
- B Theresa
- C Brock

This forest-dwelling Pokémon stores electricity in the pouches of its cheeks.

What is the name of Abigail's Pikachu?

- A Spice
- B Sweetness
- (C) Sugar

Abigail's Pikachu evolved into _Pichu_ , then learned _False_ so that it could crack open _berries_

- A Raichu, Shock Wave, Poké Balls
- (B) Raichu, Focus Punch, Aspear Berries
- C Raichu, Thunder, Ribbons

OH DO YOU KNOW THE POFFIN PLAN?

ROSERADE

Ash and friends get roped into taking a cooking class for:

A Berries

B Poffins

C Muffins

Roserade will hide the whips in its arms until it is ready to attack its foes.

They come across an expert in Poffin cooking, who also trains a Roserade. The Trainer's name is:

A Poffinnia

B Adrynnia

C Forsythia

The Roserade that battles against Team Rocket uses something to change its personality. It is a:

A Bandanna

B Wrist Bracer

C Scarf

GETTING THE PRE-CONTEST TITTERS!

PRINPLUP

Dawn's old friend who competes in the Floaroma Town Pokémon Contest is:

- **A** Kenny
- **B** Kyle
- **C** Kenji

Prinplup looks for prey in icy waters and can use its wings to break the thickest of trees.

Both Dawn and her friend are from the same location. That location is:

- **A** Twinburg Town
- **B** Two-Leaf Town
- **C** Twinleaf Town

Which evolved Pokémon does Kenny use in his showdown with Team Rocket?

- **A** Monferno
- **B** Torterra
- **C** Prinplup

DUSTOX

What does Dawn use on Pachirisu to calm it down for the Pokémon Contest?

- **A** Water
- **B** A Poké Ball
- **C** Poffin

> *When it's scared or startled, Dustox releases a toxic powder that can make you really sick. So be careful!*

Jessie uses ~~Dust x~~ in her battle with ~~dawn~~

- **A** Wobbuffet, Kenny
- **B** Dustox, Dawn
- **C** Piplup, Ash

When Dawn finally wins, she receives:

- **A** The Floaroma Ribbon
- **B** A Gym Badge
- **C** Respect

MAKE YOUR OWN TITLE!

Using the Pokémon on the left, make your own crazy Pokémon episode title — and see if you're as punny as the show's writers!

HAPPINY

MANECTRIC

BRONZONG

SUNFLORA

STARLY

MOTHIM

SHELLOS

BUDEW

SANDSHREW

RHYDON

The Taming of the _Sharix_

I Sing the Body _Karrping_

Same Old _Manectric_ and Dance!

bronzong Ever After!

Like a _Sunflora_ to the Flame!

The _Mothim_ Will Come Out Tomorrow!

Does My _Shellos_ Look Big in This?

A _budew_ Is Born!

Get _Sandshrew_, Then Get Right Off!

You Had Me at _Phydon_.

DRIFLOON ON THE WIND

DRIFLOON

On their way to Eterna City, Ash and crew stop by a Pokémon Center. The local Nurse Joy there has two daughters named:

A   Maylene and Priscilla

B   Margo and Pinkie

C   Marnie and Paige

Drifloon tries to pull on children's hands to steal them away, but it tends to be the one that gets pulled around!

The girls' father works at a company called:

A   The Ampharos Electric Company

B   The Valley Windworks Power Plant

C   Sinnoh Water and Power

A Legendary Pokémon shows up to save the day when Pikachu and one of the sisters get stuck on some nearby rocks. Which Legendary Pokémon is it?

A   Entei

B   Raikou

C   Suicune

POKÉMON FACT

POKÉMON CENTER
Each town has a place for the traveling Trainers to get medical aid for their worn-out Pokémon. Pokémon Centers are also good places for Trainers to meet other Trainers, rest, and grab a bite to eat.

THE CHAMP TWINS!

CROCONAW

Who is the lead reporter for the *Sinnoh Now!* news team?

- **A** Rhydon
- **B** Rhea
- **C** Rhonda

When battling, Croconaw will chomp down and hold on tight, even if it loses its teeth — which grow back instantly.

What are the names of the Champ Twins?

- **A** Buster and Ronnie
- **B** Billie and Richie
- **C** Brian and Ryan

Croconaw is an old Johto favorite. What other Johto Pokémon makes an appearance in this episode?

- **A** Meganium
- **B** Quilava
- **C** Ho-Oh

BURMY

Burmy can camouflage itself by burying itself in leaves and twigs.

What is the name of the Trainer who catches Burmy in the beginning of the episode?

- **A** Sherry
- **B** Sharpei
- **C** Cheryl

In addition to being a Pokémon Trainer, she also happens to be a treasure hunter. What is she looking for?

- **A** The Enchanted Honey from Amber Castle
- **B** The Golden Dew from Castle Diamante
- **C** The Silver Pollen from Beeswax Bungalow

Team Rocket also wants that Burmy, but why?

- **A** They love the way it looks
- **B** They want to evolve it into a Mothim and give it to Giovanni
- **C** They think Burmy can lead them to the treasure in the castle

THE GRASS-TYPE IS ALWAYS GREENER!

TURTWIG

Deep in the Eterna Forest, Ash and friends come across a Trainer who's a Grass-type fanatic. What's the Trainer's name and what Grass-type does she have?

Turtwig likes to live near lakes. When it drinks water, the shell on its back hardens.

   A   Garland, with a Grotle

   B   Grant, with a Torterra

   C   Gardenia, with a Turtwig

Ash tries to match the Trainer in speed and agility by sending out:

   A   Staravia, Turtwig

   B   Turtwig, Staravia

   C   Pikachu, Aipom

After Ash gets beaten by this Trainer, the Trainer offers to help them find:

   A   Mothim

   B   Combee

   C   Vespiquen

AN ANGRY COMBEENATION

COMBEE

Ash, Cheryl, and their friends finally happen upon:

- A An Enchanted Forest
- B A Combee Wall
- C A Commercial Honey Factory

Combee will collect honey for the rest of the colony and deliver it to Vespiquen.

Cheryl's Mothim has to use _____ to confuse the Combee so they don't attack.

- A Honey
- B Supersonic
- C Torment

Team Rocket's arrival sets off the hive, and it is up to _____ to fight them off.

- A Ash
- B Cheryl
- C Vespiquen

ALL DRESSED UP WITH SOMEWHERE TO GO

CROAGUNK

On their way to Eterna City, Ash and crew get caught up in:

- **A** A Team Rocket trap
- **B** A Pokémon Dress-Up Contest
- **C** A quest to save a young Trainer

The sacs on Croagonk's cheeks hold a toxic poison.

James can't help himself, and instead of finishing what he started honestly, he decides to steal:

- **A** A Pokémon
- **B** A prize Egg
- **C** A badge

Who actually is awarded the item that James tries to steal?

- **A** Ash and Turtwig
- **B** Brock and Croagunk
- **C** Dawn and Pachirisu

POKÉMON FACT

BROCK
Brock has passion for Pokémon and falls head over heels in love with every pretty girl he meets! Brock is the Gym Leader of Pewter City, and with Bonsly and Croagunk as part of his Pokémon arsenal, you'll have to agree that Brock rocks!

BUIZEL YOUR WAY OUT OF THIS

BUIZEL

Just before arriving in Eterna City, Ash and friends try to catch a Buizel. Who joins them . . . again?

A   Misty

B   May

C   Zoey

The sac around Buizel's neck acts like an inner tube, which allows it to float with its head above water. It moves by spinning its tail like a propeller.

Ash's Turtwig cuts Buizel loose from a Team Rocket net using what move?

A   Razor Wind

B   Razor Leaf

C   Hyper Cutter

Who finally gets to take Buizel as his or her own Pokémon?

A   Ash

B   Brock

C   Dawn

BRONZONG

At the Pokémon Center, our fearless adventurers meet a Trainer who specializes in Psychic-type Pokémon. That Trainer is:

   Ⓐ   Lucario

   Ⓑ   Lucinda

   Ⓒ   Lucian

In ancient times, this Pokémon was known as the bringer of plentiful harvests because it produced rain clouds.

This Trainer also belongs to a special organization called:

   Ⓐ   The B-Button League

   Ⓑ   The Eterna City Gym Leader

   Ⓒ   The Sinnoh Elite Four

Buizel has a problem that it must overcome in order to compete. That is:

   Ⓐ   Buizel can't stand being in a Poké Ball

   Ⓑ   Buizel can't accept defeat

   Ⓒ   Buizel is afraid of heights

SPELL CHECK

Mixed in with this list of legitimate Pokémon are a few that are misspelled. Being the awesome Trainer that you are, can you spot the misspelled Pokémon?

GARCHOMP	HIPPOTAS	MURKROW
SHINX	MOTHIM	PACHARISU
SHEILDON	TORTERA	URSARING
PRINPLUP	MANTINE	BLISSEY
STARAVIA	METAGROSS	MISMAGEIUS
BRONSONG	SHELLOS	CHANCEY
ELEKID	KRICETUNE	MANECTRIC
ELEKTRIKE	WEAVILE	BEEDRILL

A SECRET SPHERE OF INFLUENCE

MISDREAVUS

Help! Someone has robbed the:

A   Eterna City Bank

B   Eterna City Pokémon Zoo

C   Eterna City Historical Museum

This Ghost-type Pokémon loves to sneak up on people and scare them jus to watch their reactions.

This past acquaintance turns out to be the Eterna City Gym Leader.

A   Gardenia

B   Nando

C   Landis

The thieves made off with the _____, which increases _____'s power!

A   Eternal Orb, Palkia

B   Adamant Orb, Dialga

C   Glow Orb, Glameow

POKÉMON FACT

GYM LEADERS

The Gym Leader is usually the best Pokémon Trainer in town. Defeating a Gym Leader in a match is the only way to earn a Pokémon badge. It takes eight badges to qualify to compete in the Pokémon regional championships, where the best of the best take on each other.

CHERUBI

The Eterna City Gym contest is finally under way! In which order do the Pokémon between Ash and Gardenia win?

The small ball attached to Cherubi holds all the nutrition it needs to evolve.

- A   Staravia, Turtwig, Turtwig
- B   Aipom, Roserade, Staravia
- C   Cherubi, Staravia, Turtwig

Team Rocket keeps busy by digging for treasure when they meet:

- A   A Diglett Trainer
- B   An Underground Explorer
- C   Giovanni

Ash wins the Eterna City Gym Battle and receives the _____ Badge.

- A   Grass
- B   Flower
- C   Forest

ONE BIG HAPPINY FAMILY

HAPPINY

Where does the Cycling Road lead to?

- Ⓐ Your destiny . . .
- Ⓑ Hearthome City
- Ⓒ Lake Verity

Happiny likes to find round white rocks and carry them in its pouch so it looks like Chansey.

Jessie wants to see the stolen Happiny evolve into _____.

- Ⓐ Jigglypuff
- Ⓑ Chansey
- Ⓒ Blissey

Ash and the crew tries to cheer up someone with a serious case of the blues. Who is it?

- Ⓐ Officer Joy
- Ⓑ Nurse Jenny
- Ⓒ Nurse Joy

STEAMBOAT WILLIES

MANTINE

On their way to Hearthome City, our friends decide to take a sight-seeing trip on a:

- A Mystery Train
- B Double-Decker Bus
- C Steamboat

Mantine love to swim in open water in big groups.

Team Rocket is already on this mode of transportation, and they decide to fool the Pokémon Ash, Dawn, and Brock have left behind with:

- A Food and drink
- B Song and dance
- C Tricks and magic

The boat is headed for a giant waterfall! Ash and Dawn catch up with the help of:

- A Croagunk
- B Lapras
- C Mantine

TRAINER MATCH

Match the Trainer with the Pokémon he or she used this season.

BROCK _____

JAMES _____

ROARK _____

ZOEY _____

MARIO _____

DAWN _____

DAWN _____

PAUL _____

NANDO _____

ASH _____

PAUL _____

LANDIS _____

TOP·DOWN TRAINING

GARCHOMP

What title does Cynthia hold in Hearthome City?

- A   Grand Master Elite
- B   Master League Champion
- C   Pokémon League Champion

By spreading its wings and folding up its body, Garchomp can fly as fast as jet planes.

During the decisive first battle, which of Paul's Pokémon does Cynthia *not* knock out?

- A   Chimchar
- B   Torterra
- C   Ursaring

After Paul discovers Team Rocket is trying to kidnap Chimchar, he uses his last Pokémon's _____ to knock them out.

- A   Rock Smash move
- B   Strength attack
- C   Hyper Beam

A STAND-UP SIT-DOWN

SHELLOS

EAST SEA

WEST SEA

Shellos's body will adapt to wherever it decides to live, which is usually near water.

On the way to Hearthome City, Dawn meets up with Zoey, an old friend and rival, who's picked up a new Pokémon, a:

- **A** Bronzong
- **B** Cherrim
- **C** Shellos

Zoey informs Dawn that there's a new rule in the upcoming contest:

- **A** No Pokémon ending in the letter "e" can compete
- **B** All Pokémon will now be judged on grooming styles
- **C** It will be a double performance — two Pokémon at once!

Zoey ends up facing Jessalina in the finals, and battles:

- **A** Glameow and Shellos against Dustox and Seviper
- **B** Weavile and Shellos against Dustox and Wobbuffet
- **C** Shellos and Purugly against Dustox and Meowth

THE ELECTRIKE COMPANY

ELECTRIKE

In this episode, we meet a new Trainer named _____, who's a Pokémon breeder.

   Ⓐ   Jaco

   Ⓑ   Jacob

   Ⓒ   Jackson

This Pokémon gains reaction speed by stimulating its muscles via electricity stored in its fur.

In a strange turn of events, the only member of Team Rocket who wants to steal Electrike is:

   Ⓐ   Jessie

   Ⓑ   James

   Ⓒ   Meowth

Another awesome Evolution occurs in this episode! It is:

   Ⓐ   Electrike to Elekid

   Ⓑ   Electrike to Manectric

   Ⓒ   Pikachu to Raichu

POKÉMON FACT

MEOWTH
The talking feline that makes up one-third of Team Rocket, Meowth shows a level of intelligence far above both Jessie and James.

MALICE IN WONDERLAND

MISMAGIUS

Everyone's dream comes true in a hypnotic oasis created by Mismagius. Which of these dreams DOESN'T occur?

   A   Brock is surrounded by Nurse Joys and Officer Jennys

   B   Dawn is invited to compete in a contest of World's Best Coordinators

   C   Ash finally beats Gary in a one-on-one match

While most of Mismagius's chants can cause pain and headaches, some of them are known to bring happiness.

When Brock finally realizes that everything is not as it seems, Mismagius sends out _____ to prevent our team from waking up.

   A   Groudon

   B   Kyogre

   C   Rayquaza

Which three Pokémon grow to gigantic proportions to defeat the Mismagius illusion?

   A   Piplup, Chimchar, and Turtwig

   B   Pikachu, Croagunk, and Piplup

   C   Chimchar, Pachirisu, and Buizel

POKÉMON FACT

OFFICER JENNY

Officer Jenny is the cheerful, peacekeeping police officer. She is brave and has a strong sense of justice. Like Nurse Joy, she has a number of relatives who look exactly like her and do exactly the same job in various towns and cities.

MASS HIP·PO·SIS

HIPPOPOTAS

What is the move that Hippopotas uses in its first encounter with Team Rocket?

  A Sleep

  B Rest

  C Yawn

Hippopotas does not like getting wet. It will cover itself with sand to protect itself from water.

The attack doesn't stop Team Rocket, it just slows them down. Once they lure Hippopotas into the balloon, it uses another attack:

  A Sand Tomb

  B Take Down

  C Earthquake

Team Rocket rarely give up, even when the odds are against them. To cover up their bumbling antics, they disguise themselves as:

  A Desert tribesmen

  B Sand salesmen

  C Zoo keepers

ILL-WILL HUNTING

SHIELDON

Near _____, we find Pokémon Hunter J's goons trying to capture a Shieldon.

- A Hearthome City
- B Mt. Coronet
- C Oreburgh Mines

Shieldon constantly polishes its face by rubbing it against tree trunks. It is said that this Rock-and-Steel-type lived in jungles around a hundred million years ago.

Ash meets up with an old friend and rival, _____, who also happens to be the _____.

- A Paul, mayor of Hearthome City
- B Landis, president of the Pokétch Corporation
- C Gary, grandson of Professor Oak

This old rival irritates a hive of _____ in order to create a distraction and get away from Pokémon Hunter J's crew.

- A Combee
- B Shedinja
- C Beedrill

SINNOH WORD SEARCH, PART II

Okay, Trainers and Coordinators,
here's another word search for you!
The following characters were featured in
Pokémon: Diamond and Pearl. *Can you find them all?*
You can search down, up, forward, backward, and diagonally.

CLARA

FORSYTHIA

GARDENIA

GARY

HALEY

HOLLY

JESSALINA

JOHANNA

LANDIS

MINNIE

MIRA

NANDO

ORALIE

PAUL

PRINCESS
POWERZONE

ROARK

ZOEY

```
E I Y P I I E N K D Y N B S L N
N Y R I E N Z R A I L P N S A K
O N A Y N A F D K A N O A Y A E
Z R E A C T T E R J C G R O I O
R A O A Y S L I A N L R A Y Z T
E C O F R Y L L O H N A E A G F
W A A O O A G A R D E N I A Y I
O I A S W R E R N A T N R E L U
P U O T E Q S O V I L Y E K I M
S A O T N Y D Y H F L G N E J T
S O D N A N Z W T U L A N D I S
E D A E A Y E L A H E L S F A H
C L A R A S L P R R I E F S Y S
N O B N A K S O L A N A E A E N
I S N J R A H A R A N N A H O J
R Y S R S G A I A Y I N N Y Z A
P A T R D W M L E N M I A S I H
```

STARAVIA

Dawn is rushing through the forest because:

A   A contest is about to start at the Pokémon Center

B   She needs to turn in a coupon at the Pokémon Center

C   She really has to use the bathroom at the Pokémon Center

Staravia fly around in flocks. They hunt in the forests and plains they call home for Bug-type Pokémon.

During their adventures here, the team is split up when _____ are chased by _____.

A   Geodude and Diglett, Steelix

B   Golem and Graveler, Onix

C   Dugtrio and Sandshrew, Rhydon

The coupon that Dawn turned in was for:

A   A free stay at the Pokémon Day Care Center

B   A free dinner at the Hearthome City Mall

C   A Coin-Toss Pokétch Application

SANDSHREW'S LOCKER

SANDSHREW

Ash and his crew are approached by a young girl named _____, who has a _____ with her.

This Pokémon curls into a defensive ball when attacked.

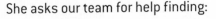

   A   Sandra, Sandshrew

   B   Mary, Sandslash

   C   Mira, Abra

She asks our team for help finding:

   A   A shortcut

   B   Heirloom jewelry

   C   A magical mirror

All this searching for lost things turns out to be a ruse to help her get a Pokémon back from a submerged underwater city. That Pokémon is:

   A   Sandslash

   B   Cacturne

   C   Sandshrew

DAWN'S EARLY NIGHT

KRICKETUNE

The crew has reached Hearthome City at last, but no Gym Leader is available right now. Still, there is a Pokémon Contest, and the Coordinators are:

- **A** Dawn, Nando, Zoey, Jessalina
- **B** Dawn, Ash, Brock, Jessalina
- **C** Dawn, Zoey, Jessalina, Paul

Kricketune shows its emotion by creating melodies. When it cries, it crosses its arms in front of itself.

The first contestant up is:

- **A** Dawn with Pachirisu and Piplup
- **B** Zoey with Glameow and Shellos
- **C** Nando with Sunflora and Kricketune

Who defeats whom in the finals?

- **A** Dawn defeats Jessalina
- **B** Zoey defeats Nando
- **C** Nando defeats Zoey

TAG! WE'RE IT

WINGULL

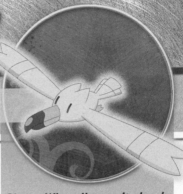

Who is the sly and devious Trainer with Slowking?

- **A** Conrad
- **B** Confucius
- **C** Conway

Clever Wingull uses its beak to carry valuables until it can hide them away.

The prize in the Tag Battle Tournament is:

- **A** The Soothe Bell
- **B** The Ice Badge
- **C** The Hearthome City Key

Which Pokémon ISN'T in the Tag Tournament?

- **A** Yanma
- **B** Koffing
- **C** Aggron

GLORY BLAZE

CHIMCHAR

Paul reminisces about finding Chimchar, which was being cornered by a group of:

- **A** Children
- **B** Zangoose
- **C** Turtwig

Even rain can't put out Chimchar's fiery tail.

In the next tag battle, Paul and Chimchar face that Pokémon plus one other:

- **A** Beldum
- **B** Metang
- **C** Metagross

The battle becomes one of fearful memories for Chimchar. After the battle, Paul:

- **A** Berates Chimchar for a poor performance
- **B** Watches as an angry Chimchar evolves into Monferno
- **C** Releases Chimchar in disgust

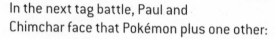

SMELLS LIKE TEAM SPIRIT

TORTERRA

In the finals of the Hearthome City Tag Battles, Brock successfully teams up with a female trainer. Her name is:

Smaller Pokémon sometimes build nests on the backs of Torterra.

A   Holly

B   Harriet

C   Hilda

After beating Brock and his partner,
Ash and Paul move on to Dawn and her partner, _____ ,who
battles with a _____ .

A   Conrad, Hippopotas

B   Conway, Heracross

C   Constantine, Hariyama

We get to see an unbelievable Evolution! It is:

A   Pikachu into Raichu

B   Staravia into Staraptor

C   Elekid into Electabuzz

ANSWERS

Give yourself one point for every correct answer.

pg 6: C, B, C; **pg 7:** A, E, B;

Sinnoh Sudoku! **pgs 8–9**

pg 10: B, B, A; **pg 11:** B, A, C; **pg 12:** C, C, A; **pg 13:** B, C, A

It's a Map, Map, Map World **pgs 14–15**

		A	S	H		
	N	E	V	E	R	
G	I	V	E	S	U	P

pg 16: C, C, B; **pg 17:** B, B, A; **pg 18:** A, B, C; **pg 19:** A, B, C

Anagram Madness! **pgs 20–21**

1. Pikachu
2. Buneary
3. Pachirisu
4. Croagunk
5. Team Rocket
6. Ludicolo
7. Elekid
8. Aipom
9. Wormadam
10. Staravia

pg 22: C, C, A; **pg 23:** C, C, C; **pg 24:** C, A, A; **pg 25:** B, C, C

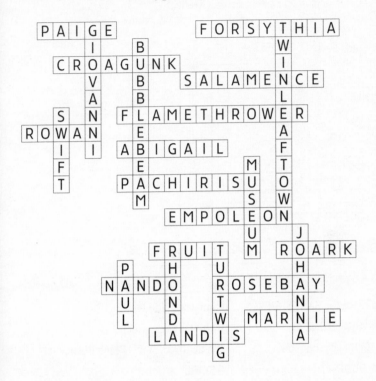

pg 28: B, B, C; **pg 29:** C, C, C; **pg 30:** C, C, C; **pg 31:** B, B, B

Evolution Solution **pgs 32–33**

1.	2	1	3	5. 2	3	1
2.	1	3	2	6. 3	1	2
3.	3	1	2	7. 1	2	3
4.	1	2	3	8. 3	1	2

pg 34: C, B, B; **pg 35:** C, B, A; **pg 36:** C, C, C; **pg 37:** C, C, B

Word Search **pgs 38–39**

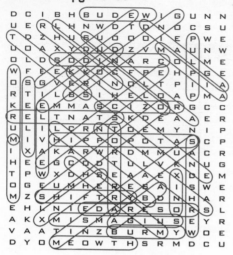

pg 40: B, C, B; **pg 41:** B, C, C; **pg 42:** A, C, C; **pg 43:** C, B, A

Make Your Own Title! **pgs 44–45**

The Taming of the **SANDSHREW**

Same Old **BRONZONG** and Dance!

Like a **MOTHIM** to the Flame!

Does My **BUDEW** Look Big in This?

Get **RHYDON**, Then Get Right Off!

I Sing the Body **MANECTRIC**

HAPPINY Ever After!

The **SUNFLORA** Will Come Out Tomorrow!

A **STARLY** Is Born!

You Had Me at **SHELLOS**!

pg 46: C, B, C; **pg 47:** C, C, B; **pg 48:** C, A, B; **pg 49:** C, B, B

pg 50: B, B, C; **pg 51:** B, B, B; **pg 52:** C, B, C; **pg 53:** C, C, B

Spell Check **pgs 54–55**

GARCHOMP	HIPPOTAS	MURKROW
SHINX	MOTHIM	PACHARISU
SHEILDON	TORTERA	URSARING
PRINPLUP	MANTINE	BLISSEY
STARAVIA	METAGROSS	MISMAGEIUS
BRONSONG	SHELLOS	CHANCEY
ELEKID	KRICETUNE	MANECTRIC
ELEKTRIKE	WEAVILE	BEEDRILL

pg 56: C, A, B; **pg 57:** A, B, C; **pg 58:** B, B, C; **pg 59:** C, B, C

Trainer Match **pgs 60–61**

POKÉMON	TRAINER	POKÉMON	TRAINER
Pachirisu	Dawn	Piplup	Dawn
Elekid	Paul	Gardevoir	Mario
Budew	Nando	Shinx	Landis
Geodude	Roark	Glameow	Zoey
Turtwig	Ash	Carnivine	James
Chimchar	Paul	Croagunk	Brock

pg 62: C, C, C; **pg 63:** C, C, A; **pg 64:** A, A, B;
pg 65: C, C, B; **pg 66:** C, A, B; **pg 67:** B, C, C

Sinnoh Word Search, Part II **pgs 68–69**

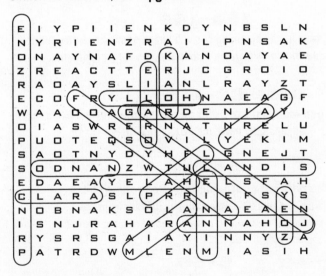

pg 70: B, B, C; **pg 71:** C, B, C; **pg 72:** A, C, C; **pg 73:** C, A, C;
pg 74: B, C, C; **pg 75:** A, B, C

SCORING

150 AND ABOVE
You don't need to read this guide — you should write a guide!

120–149
You are definitely in the running for a Trainer position. Good work — you have made everyone in the Sinnoh Region proud!

90–119
Not bad, but you may want to build up your knowledge a little more before you venture out into Sinnoh.

80–89
You only got about half the questions right, which means you need to study a little more. Don't despair — it takes a lot of work to be a Trainer!

0–59
Ummm . . . maybe you're not in this for the whole knowledge, "I-want-to-be-a-professor" sort of thing.